Sky Pony Press books may be purchased in bulk at special discounts for sales promotion, corporate gifts, fund-raising, or educational purposes. Special editions can also be created to specifications. For details, contact the Special Sales Department, Sky Pony Press, 307 West 36th Street, 11th Floor, New York, NY 10018 or info@skyhorsepublishing.com.

Sky Pony® is a registered trademark of Skyhorse Publishing, Inc.®, a Delaware corporation.

Visit our website at www.skyponypress.com.

10 9 8 7 6 5 4 3 2 1

Manufactured in China, May 2012
This product conforms to CPSIA 2008

Mueller, Dagmar H.
[David's Welt. English]
David's world : a picture book about living with autism / Dagmar H. Mueller ;
illustrations by Verena Ballhaus.
p. cm.
Summary: A young boy's understanding of his autistic brother, David, improves as a therapist works with the family to better interpret David's behavior, and with David to communicate through words.
ISBN 978-1-61608-962-7 (hardcover : alk. paper)
[1. Autism--Fiction. 2. Brothers--Fiction. 3. Communication--Fiction. 4. Family life--Fiction.] I. Ballhaus, Verena, ill. II. Title.
PZ7.M8785Dav 2012
[E]--dc23
2012010534

Dagmar H. Mueller

David's World

A Picture Book about Living with Autism

With Illustrations by Verena Ballhaus

Translated by Kim Gardner

Sky Pony Press
New York

David

David doesn't like it when I'm noisy. He likes it even less when I hug him. He doesn't like it at all when I bring a lot of friends home. He goes straight to his room and closes the door behind him, to make sure he doesn't see or hear us.

Sometimes I don't like David. He's so different.

He speaks a different language. He doesn't act like me or Mom or Dad or all the other people I know. He doesn't laugh when we laugh, and he doesn't cry when he's sad.

Sometimes he gets mad, and sometimes he doesn't talk to anyone all day.

But usually, I like David. Because David is my brother.

Is my brother an alien?

My best friend, Josh, says that David's an alien. He believes that David comes from a different planet and just accidentally fell out of a spaceship and straight into our family by chance. And sometimes Josh even says we better send David back to his own planet. To the place where everyone is just like David and speaks the same language. Josh thinks that David would definitely be happier there.

But that won't work! We can't just drop David on another planet. I'm really sure that Josh is just making this up. After all, David is my brother!

And he shouldn't live anywhere else!

And mostly, I know for sure that David enjoys living with us. Very much, actually. Even if it doesn't look that way. David wouldn't like to be anywhere else. He told me so himself.

David speaks a different language

On good days, David talks with us. In our language.

Sometimes, David says funny things, though, or says things in a strange way. So, sometimes I don't really understand him. And I know that he often doesn't really understand me.

When I'm happy and scream "Hooray!" out loud and run up to David and want to hug him, he looks really mad and doesn't think that's funny at all.

Sometimes David stretches out right between me and the TV and just looks right in my face without saying a word. Of course, then I growl angrily at him, "Go away!"

David can really be a pain.

But he just wants to say "hello" and to ask me in his language if he can watch with me.

But that's how it is—Mom says—when you speak different languages. There are a lot of misunderstandings.

That's true. I remember how it was when all of us were in France on vacation. There, Dad tried really hard to be understood in French when speaking. And the people in France also tried really hard to understand Dad. But now and then, they laughed or even tapped themselves gently on their foreheads, and maybe thought that Dad was a little crazy. That's because Dad wasn't able to speak what he wanted to say the right way in the foreign language.

What I wish

It's like that with David too. He
still doesn't get to say what he'd like to say. But
he wants to tell us something. Very much. And he's doing
that more and more.

I wish I could understand David's language even better.
I wish David would master our language even better.
I wish I could take a peek inside David's world at least once and feel
what David feels.
I wish David could be just like us for one day and tell us everything
and show us everything he wants to, and what he thinks, and what he's
capable of—everything that we unfortunately don't see.

Sometimes David is angry

David gets angry fits. It used to be worse than it is now.

The more he learns to speak our language, the less often he has to get mad.

Before, David would get mad over the smallest things. Over such small things that Mom or Dad or I usually didn't notice. That could be annoying sometimes.

He would get mad if Mom moved around the furniture in the living room. David doesn't like changes.

David likes it when the same thing happens every day, when he's in the same place every day, and when that place looks the same every day.

Who would have thought that you could get mad if Mom moves a chair? But that is bad for David.

David also likes to have the same food every day, and when he reads or hears something, he often repeats certain sentences from it all week long. Over and over again.

David just doesn't like what's new.

David, Mom, Dad, and I are learning

Before, David would usually get mad if we didn't realize what he wanted.

That's easy to understand. I'll get mad too, if Mom or Josh or Dad doesn't figure out what I want. I think they're really stupid and could try a little more.

The silly thing was just that Mom or Dad or I usually didn't notice at all that David wanted to help us. It's really just that his language is so different from ours. That is, he spoke just a little with words before. He spoke in a language that we didn't understand.

But now, Mom, Dad, David, and I are learning. We're learning with Mara. Mara is a therapist and very nice. She practices our language with David, so that he can talk with our words too. And she explains David's language to Mom and Dad and me, so we can understand him when he doesn't find the words.

Sometimes David is sad

David now says, "The light is too bright," when Mom turns on
the lamp. Then he leaves the room. It's good that David can say
that now. Who would have thought that David must leave a room
just because Mom had turned on the lamp? But bright light is too
harsh and uncomfortable for him.

David also says, "The coffeemaker is too loud," and jumps from
the table and runs in his room and locks the door, as if he is afraid
that the coffeemaker can follow him.

Yes, it's very good that David can say that now. Because Mom
didn't understand before how awful it was for David to listen to
a noise like that, and she would make him stay sitting as usual at
the table with us. And that would have been bad for David. Almost
like if someone made me mad by making me stand next to a loud
siren on a fire engine. Who would like that? That really hurts! So of
course David would get mad.

Sometimes David says nothing and goes away without a word. And when that happens he's usually sad. Because he didn't find a way to tell us something.

David and I don't like the same things

Mara says, "David gets mad when he's scared or when he isn't understood, or when he wants something someone else won't give him."

And it works just like that with me. Except that the things I want and the things that David wants are as different as day and night, or as English and Chinese, or as words and pictures.

For example, I like to play soccer.

David doesn't like playing soccer. There are too many people for him. David prefers to be alone. Most sports are just too wild for him. David prefers everything arranged nicely. And in order.

David likes to play piano. He listens to pieces on the radio and plays them back.

Without music. Right away. Without practicing. He can listen super well. Much better than I can.

Sometimes I just plop down on the carpet and listen to David as he plays and plays and plays.

David feels. A lot.

David says that he sees much more and hears much more than we do. That he notices things that we don't notice. He says the world rushes through his head like a hurricane so that he has to relax from it more than we do.

Once I was with David in the shopping mall as the hurricane rushed. David was very tense. His face was gloomy and defensive. And suddenly, I could see and hear the storm myself.

First, the bright-red honking sports car rushed by us in front of the entrance with yelling boys in it. At the same time, lightning fired down on us from the lights on the other side of the ice cream shop, a loudspeaker announcement thundered right into our heads, and two arguing, fighting guys raged right through the middle of our bodies, while a woman shaking our arms wanted to know the time.

Waves of screaming babies in strollers swirled away over us,
glaring bright neon signs jumped painfully in our faces from
all directions, and each store entrance mercilessly shot cannons
of music at us until our ears were totally worn out.

It was just too much!

David can observe well

David hears things that we don't hear and sees things that we don't see.

One time, we were over at our neighbor Sabine's house with Mom and Dad so we could meet Sabine's new dog Murmel. Mom had brought along flowers and Sabine baked cake, but we didn't get to eat anything because Murmel barked and barked and barked the whole time.

He didn't bark at us. He barked at the table.

"What is wrong with him?" Sabine asked, without a clue, and even offered Murmel some cake to calm him down.

But Murmel didn't calm down.
He kept barking again and again.
Mom and Dad and I tried
everything. We petted him, we put him
on our laps, but nothing helped.

Murmel barked at the table.

David can understand animals

"QUIET!" Dad finally said in his energetic dad-tone. But Murmel didn't look at Dad. Murmel only looked at the table and barked.

David did nothing. He didn't pet Murmel, and he didn't say anything to him. David observed Murmel.

And he observed the table.

And then David stood up and went to the table.

And he quietly took the flower vase from the table and put it outside on the windowsill.

And Murmel stopped barking and followed David thankfully with his eyes. Then he sat down on his little behind, panting, exhausted from barking, smiled at us, and happily wagged his tail.

Sabine's jaw dropped in amazement.

"He was scared," David said. "Of the flowers. The flowers were not good. Now, everything is okay again."

And that was it. David made everything okay. David can understand animals better than anyone I know.

David is autistic

Some people think that David isn't really smart, because he says so little. And because he understands some things totally wrong.

That just means that he speaks a different language than we do.

Because David is autistic. And some people are just too dumb to realize that.

Being autistic is not a career or anything like that. It's not a skin color either, or nationality, or sickness where you get a fever or lose your hair.

To be autistic means to live in your own world. And that feels comfortable for David.

You aren't autistic because you want to be, or because you didn't wear enough clothes in the biggest snowstorm, or because you might have an allergic reaction to green cabbage. You are autistic from birth. But sometimes the people around you don't notice it until much later.

For me, David is not even autistic.

For me, David is just my brother.

And he is someone really special!